written & illustrated by Mercer Mayer

What do you do

with a kangaroo?

SCHOLASTIC STARLINE EDITION
Scholastic Book Services
New York   Toronto   London   Auckland   Sydney   Tokyo

A hardcover edition of this book is published by Four Winds Press, a division of Scholastic Magazines, Inc., and is available through your local bookstore or directly from Four Winds Press, 50 West 44th Street, New York, New York 10036.

Copyright © 1973 by Mercer Mayer
All rights reserved. This StarLine edition is published by Scholastic Book Services, a division of Scholastic Magazines, Inc.

13 12 11 10 9 8 7 6 5 4 3 2   7 8 9/7 01/8

07

For Pat

What do you do with a Kangaroo
    who jumps in your window, sits on your bed,
    and says,
    "I never sleep on wrinkled sheets,
    so change them now and make them smooth,
    and fluff up the pillows if you please."

What do you do?

You throw him out, that's what you do.
"Get out of my bed, you Kangaroo!"

What do you do when you go to the bathroom
  to wash your face,
  And hanging there where your towel should be,
  brushing his teeth like he owns the place
  is an Opossum?
He says to you, "This toothpaste you use is much
  too sweet,
  and your toothbrush, I'm sorry to say,
  is all worn.
  Please get me a new one tomorrow."

What do you do?

You grab him up by his skinny tail
and carry him off, that's what you do.
"Get out of my bathroom, you Opossum!"

What do you do if you want to get dressed,
    but wearing your jeans, your favorite pair,
    is a Llama, who says,
    "I lost my pants on the tennis court —
    I think yours will do, though the color's all wrong?
    The knees are tight, and a button is gone,

the cuffs are frayed, and for goodness sake,
the seam is ripped—so send these right off
to the tailor."

What do you do?

You throw him out, that's what you do.

"Gimmie my pants back, you Llama!"

What do you do when you go down to eat,
and there on the table dipping his paws
in your cereal bowl is a smiling Raccoon?
"This cereal is stale," he says to you,
"but I'm so hungry that I don't care,
and I never eat with dirty paws, so
bring me a gold-plated finger bowl
and fill it with water of scented rose.
And bring me a towel of fluffy lamb's wool
and a whisker brush too, for I'm very neat.
And hurry! I've been waiting all morning!"

What do you do?

You throw him out, it's as simple as that.

"Stay away from my breakfast, you Raccoon!"

What do you do if you want to go out
   but there in the doorway blocking your view
   stands a large baby Moose?
"I won't move," she explains, "till you give me a bath
   in apricot juice, and brush my teeth
   with a sassafras root,
   and play me a tune on a brass French horn,
   and say 'pretty-please' fifteen times."

What do you do?

You throw her out, that's what you do.

"Get out of my way, you old Moose, you!"

What do you do if you want to go riding
    but there on your red-painted tricycle seat
    sits a grown Bengal Tiger with flashing green eyes?
"Hurry up," he exclaims, "and push me along
    to the Taj Mahal Circus before it's too late.
    You'll have to push fast and sing me a song
    about waffles and airplanes and matters-of-fact.
    And when we arrive, just to show you my thanks—
    I'll *eat* you for dinner or breakfast!"

What do you do?

Give that Tiger a push, if that's what he wants.
You push him right off, that's all there is to it.

"Get off of my tricycle, you Tiger!"

What do you do if you fill up the tub
    but before you get wet
    a Camel comes in and drinks the tub dry?
Then chewing your washcloth, he says with a burp,
    "Now fill up the tub, I've a terrible thirst,
    and throw in some tasty bath salt, if you please.
    But this time, leave out the soap."

What do you do?

You throw him out, that's what you do.

"Get away from my bathtub, you Camel!"

What do you do if it's late at night
    but all snuggled up where you always sleep
    is a Camel, a Moose, a Llama, an Opossum,
    a Tiger, a Raccoon, and a Kangaroo?
And all at once they say to you,
    "We're very sorry if you want to sleep,
    but as you can see there's no more room.
    So make some warm milk and bring us a glass,
    find some more blankets—it's chilly in here—
    and remember the chocolate chip cookies."

Now I'll say it again: *What do you do?*

Well, you know what to do.

You throw them all out, that's what you do!

What do you do if you can't throw them out?

You let them stay.